MONKEY GOES TO HOSPITAL

Written by Sue Graves

Illustrated by Trevor Dunton

W
FRANKLIN WATTS
LONDON•SYDNEY

Monkey was very excited! Lion and Giraffe had come to play. Dad said they could play outside. Monkey asked if they could climb the big tree.

Dad said yes, but they had to be careful! He said they had to hold on tight and **be sensible**!

Monkey got to the tree first. He climbed really high. Lion and Giraffe told him to be careful. They told him to hold on tight.

But Monkey **didn't listen.**
He started to **show off**.

Lion and Giraffe told Monkey to **stop being silly**.
They said he would fall if he didn't hold on tight.

But Monkey didn't listen. He showed off even more! He forgot to hold on tight. He fell down with a **loud thump**!

Lion and Giraffe ran to help him. Monkey was upset. He felt very dizzy. His leg hurt too. Lion and Giraffe were worried.

10

Giraffe ran to get Dad.

Dad said he had better take Monkey to hospital for a check-up. But Monkey didn't want to go to hospital. He didn't want a check-up at all. He said hospitals were scary!

13

Then Lion told Monkey that he hurt his head once at his granny's house. He said he had to go to hospital. He felt scared.

But his granny said hospitals were **good places**.
She said the doctors and nurses were kind and
would help him.

Lion said he was scared when they put a big bandage on his head. But he thought of **nice things** to take his mind off it.
He said that helped a lot!

The doctor said he was a **very brave** lion.
Lion said he felt proud.

Monkey had a think. He wanted to be brave like Lion. He said he could think of nice things to take his mind off it.

Dad said that was a **good idea**.

At the hospital, a nurse took Monkey's temperature.
He said his temperature was very good.
Monkey was pleased.

Next, a doctor looked in his eyes. She felt his head and his leg, too.

Then the doctor said Monkey needed an X-ray to make sure his leg was alright. She said an X-ray was like having a picture taken. Monkey didn't want an X-ray. He said an X-ray sounded **scary**.

Then he remembered what Lion said. He thought about lots of nice things. Soon the X-ray was done ... and it **didn't hurt** at all. The doctor said Monkey was very brave. Monkey was **proud**.

The doctor told Monkey that he had sprained his leg. She said she would put a bandage on it to help it **get better**. She said he would have to rest his leg for a few days.

Monkey was pleased with his bandage.
Best of all, the doctor gave him a sticker.

Monkey showed Lion and Giraffe his bandage and his sticker. Monkey said he hoped he could climb the tree again soon. But next time, he promised to hold on and **not show off**. Everyone said that was **a very good idea**!

A note about sharing this book

The *Experiences Matter* series has been developed
to provide a starting point for further
discussion on how children might deal
with new experiences. It provides
opportunities to explore ways of
developing coping strategies as they
face new challenges.

The series is set in the jungle with
animal characters reflecting typical
behaviour traits and attitudes often
seen in young children.

Monkey Goes to Hospital
This story looks at some of the typical reasons why children may be
nervous if they have to go to hospital. It highlights coping strategies they
might use in such situations.

How to use the book
The book is designed for adults to share with either an individual child,
or a group of children, and as a starting point for discussion.

The book also provides visual support and repeated words and phrases
to build reading confidence.

Before reading the story
Choose a time to read when you and the children are relaxed and have
time to share the story.

Spend time looking at the illustrations and talk about what the book
might be about before reading it together.

Encourage children to employ a phonics-first approach to tackling
new words by sounding the words out.

After reading, talk about the book with the children:

- After reading the book together, invite the children to retell the story in their own words in chronological order.

- Use the book as a starting point for discussion on Monkey's behaviour. Do the children agree that Monkey was silly to show off? Why do they think he was showing off in the first place?

- What do the children think about the way Lion and Giraffe dealt with the situation? Do they agree that it was wise for Lion to stay with Monkey while Giraffe went to get help? Why?

- Talk about the strategies that Lion suggests and Monkey subsequently uses to allay his fears when going to the hospital. Have any of the children been in a similar situation? How did they cope? Encourage the children to share their experiences.

Remind the children to listen carefully while others speak and to wait for their turn.

- Invite the children to draw a picture of nice things they could think about if they were in a similar situation to Monkey. Ask them to write a sentence to describe their picture.

- Ask the children to write a sentence about the person they would go to for help in such a situation.

- Select children to show their work to the others and use the children's work to trigger further discussion.

For Isabelle, William A, William G, George, Max, Emily,

Leo, Caspar, Felix, Tabitha, Phoebe, Harry and Libby –S.G.

Franklin Watts
First published in 2023 by
Hodder & Stoughton

Text © Hodder & Stoughton Limited, 2023
Illustrations © Trevor Dunton, 2023

The right of Trevor Dunton to be identified as the illustrator
of this Work has been asserted in accordance with the
Copyright, Designs and Patents Act, 1988.

Editor: Jackie Hamley
Designer: Cathryn Gilbert

A CIP catalogue record for this book is available
from the British Library.

ISBN 978 1 4451 8210 0 (hardback)
ISBN 978 1 4451 8211 7 (paperback)
ISBN 978 1 4451 8872 0 (ebook)

Printed in China

Franklin Watts
An imprint of
Hachette Children's Books,
Part of Hodder & Stoughton
Carmelite House
50 Victoria Embankment
London EC4Y 0DZ

An Hachette UK company
www.hachettechildrens.co.uk